Boy on the Mayflower

By IRIS VINTON
Illustrated by JON NIELSEN

Adventures of Will Latham on the First Voyage of the Pilgrims

For more than two hundred years little was known of what really happened when the little Pilgrim band set sail for a strange and forbidding New World. Then in 1856 a searcher found in a dusty British library Governor William Bradford's own story of the "Plimoth Plantation." We know the Pilgrims brought with them 41 boys and girls. This is the story of one of those young passengers. For her facts the author relies on the true history of that first hazard-filled voyage.

SCHOLASTIC BOOK SERVICES
NEW YORK • TORONTO • LONDON • AUCKLAND • SYDNEY • TOKYO

 Published by Scholastic Book Services, a division of Scholastic Magazines, Inc.

25 24 23 22 21 20 19 18 17 16 15 6 7 8 9/7 01/8

Printed in the U.S.A. 07

WILL Latham perched in his favorite spot high in the rigging of the *Speedwell.* He watched the blue waves blossom with whitecaps. His thoughts were far across the Atlantic Ocean in America. In his imagination, he was creeping toward Indians seated around a campfire. His spine tingled at the thought.

"Man the pumps!" bellowed the voice of Captain Reynolds from somewhere beneath him. It broke into Will's daydreaming like a clap of thunder.

He looked down. Sailors ran forward to the pumps. The captain, standing near the mast, continued to bellow: "Look alive, men! This ship's leaking like a sieve!"

The men began to pump furiously. Water gushed over the deck, and poured into the sea.

In a few minutes the captain called to the men, "Let's sound. If the pumps gain on the leak, all may yet be well."

The captain let down the long sounding rod to measure the depth of the water in the hold.

He drew the rod back up.

"The water has to be lower!" Will whispered fiercely. "It has to be!"

But to his dismay, he saw Captain Reynolds shake his head. The harsh strokes of the pumps sounded again. And again water gushed up and flowed over the deck into the sea.

By now, word of the bad leak had reached all ears. The Pilgrims – men, women, and children – hurried from different parts of the ship to stand in silence, watching the crew at the pumps, with anxious faces.

Then Will saw his employer, John Carver, point excitedly to their companion ship, the *Mayflower*. All sails spread, the *Mayflower* danced ahead on the blue water.

Captain Reynolds came out of his cabin, with a spyglass under his arm. Putting the glass to his eye, he trained it on the *Mayflower*. Painted on the tall

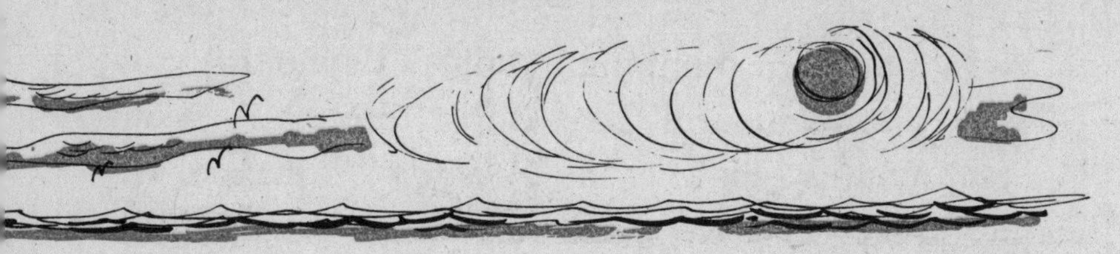

stern, the white flower with its yellow center, a mayflower, flashed in the distance like the white tail of a running deer.

"Signal the *Mayflower* to heave to!" the captain shouted across the deck to the first mate.

As the signal flag rose swiftly to the top of the gaff, Will felt fear tighten like a knot inside of him. If the *Speedwell* were forced to turn back once more the Carvers might give up all hope of going to America. Then Will Latham would be sent back to the London slums where Mr. Carver, that fine Pilgrim gentleman, had found and hired him.

Gloomily, he watched the *Mayflower* crew haul in sail. Soon the two ships lay side by side, bobbing on the waves.

Will scurried down the rigging. Racing across the deck he found a place at the rail, near Mr. Carver. Captain Reynolds called to Captain Christopher Jones: "The *Speedwell's* leaking badly again. I must put back or sink."

"We're three hundred miles out!" exclaimed the burly captain of the *Mayflower*. "Plymouth is the nearest port. Do you think you can make it?"

"Ay, with much pumping," replied Reynolds.

"Return to Plymouth!" John Carver protested. "We lost two months repairing the *Speedwell* last time. If we lose more time, we'll run into winter storms."

"Better to lose time than lose your lives," snapped Captain Reynolds.

Then came the rattling of blocks and shaking of sails as the two ships swung around. Their sails spread, they headed back to England and the nearest port, Plymouth.

Will leaned his elbows on the rail and stared at the water. He was sunk in gloom. He might as well give up his dreams of adventures in the wilderness. He would grow up a street boy in London.

Several days later the *Mayflower* and the *Speedwell* sailed into Plymouth harbor. While the Pilgrims waited, torn between hope and despair, the ship's officers examined the *Speedwell*.

Then Captain Reynolds announced the bleak news: "The leaks cannot be stopped. The ship is unseaworthy."

The Pilgrims were in despair. What would they do now? To stay in England was dangerous. They might be thrown in jail if they dared to worship God according to their Puritan faith. Some Pilgrim leaders would probably be tried for treason and hanged.

Yet how could the fifty or more from the *Speedwell*

crowd onto the already well-filled *Mayflower?* The leaders met in the captain's cabin to decide what to do.

Thirteen-year-old Will Latham wandered about the deck, waiting, waiting, waiting. His whole life depended upon what those men decided behind the closed door.

ALMOST LEFT BEHIND

AT supper that evening on the *Speedwell,* Mr. Carver broke the news to his family group—his wife, her young ward, and five employes, including Will.

"We are going to America in the *Mayflower,*" he announced in his calm voice.

Will was so relieved, he cried, "Thank heaven, sir! I had my heart set on going to America. I couldn't bear not to go, sir."

Mr. Carver smiled at him. "You've a stout heart, Will. We'll have need of it," he said, then went on. "The *Speedwell* returns to London with the people who are staying behind. The rest of us will move to the *Mayflower*."

Silence followed as each of them pondered the news. Will looked around the circle. In the short time he had known Mr. and Mrs. Carver and the others, he had come to think of them as his family. Eight altogether. And they were all going together to America. Will sighed contentedly.

At last, on September 16, 1620, the *Mayflower* was once again ready to put to sea. Boats waited at the wharf to take the last passengers out to the ship.

Mr. Carver hurried down the crowded wharf with a chest of beads and various trinkets for trading with the Indians. Will, carrying his own sea bag, a bundle of books, and Mrs. Carver's pet starling in a cage, hurried after him. In the jostle of sailors, dock hands and farm carts, Will became separated from Mr. Carver.

Looking up, Will was startled to see the *Mayflower* beginning to shake out her sails, getting ready to start.

"I must hurry," he told himself. He began to run. The cage banged against his leg, slowing him down. Just as he turned out of the way of a woman with a tray of pies, a man with a wheelbarrow loaded with

oysters ran into him. Will went sprawling.

Before he could gather up his books, bag, and birdcage, he had lost many minutes. Reaching the wharf, he saw with dismay two boats, filled with passengers, being rowed out to the *Mayflower*.

Will shouted. He jumped up and down to attract their attention. But his voice was drowned in the noise of the crowd and people calling, "Godspeed the *Mayflower!*"

He looked wildly around. Then he spied seamen in a skiff. They were big, husky fellows with skin like

brown leather. Will darted over to them.

"Please, sirs, could you row me to the *Mayflower?*" he blurted out. "I'm Mr. Carver's apprentice and I must get aboard. I missed the boat."

Roars of laughter greeted his speech. "So you missed the boat!" a sailor taunted him. "Then you shall have to swim for it."

"What's going on here?" demanded a loud, rough voice.

Will spun round. "Captain Jones!" he cried, recognizing the *Mayflower* captain. "I've been left behind. Please take me with you." He dropped his sea bag and tugged frantically at the skipper's sleeve.

"Stand aside, boy," commanded Jones. "We've more aboard now than we know what to do with," He shook Will off as though he were a puppy.

"But, Captain Jones, you can't leave me!" Will cried in desperation. "I'm Mr. Carver's apprentice. Surely, sir, you know Mr. Carver."

The captain scowled, started toward the boat, then hesitated.

"Here, I can prove it, sir," Will said. Snatching a book from the bundle under his arm, he flipped it open. "See, sir, there's Mr. Carver's name – John Carver – written in his own hand."

Jones leaned down and squinted at the page. "Ay,

that's the name of one of the Pilgrim leaders," he admitted grudgingly. He jerked his head toward the boat. "Get in and be quick about it."

SAINTS AND STRANGERS

THE skiff had barely nudged the side of the *Mayflower* when Will sprang for the rope ladder and began to climb.

"Stand clear!" cried the biggest and roughest of the sailors. At the same time, he plucked Will off the

A typical 16th century merchant ship, the *Mayflower* was 106 feet long from jutting beak to aftercastle and had a 25-foot beam. Height from keel to taffrail around the poop deck—40 feet.

KEY TO DRAWING

1. Poop deck. 2. Quarter deck.
3. Upper deck. 4. Forecastle.
5. Main deck. Here with their belongings, lived the Pilgrims.
6. Crew's quarters. 7. Bosun's store.
8. Galley, with cooking range.
9. Main hold, general cargo, barrelled beer, dried meat, etc.

Based on drawing made for Plimoth Plantation.

10. Cargo. 11. General stores.
12. Barrels of water.
13. Barrels of biscuits and flour.
14. Typical temporary cabin, made with canvas, bulkheads/partitions.
15. Special cabins–two each side.
16. Tiller room.
17. Helmsman, with whipstaff connection to tiller. No steering wheel yet.
18. Captain's "Great Room."
19. Pens for livestock. 20. Beak.
21. Bowsprit.
22. Foremast. 23. Mainmast.
24. Mizzenmast.

ropes and flung him back into the skiff.

"The captain goes first, ye ignorant landlubber whelp," he said angrily, giving Will a kick that made him wince.

"Let be!" barked Captain Jones, scowling at the rough sailor. "You're altogether too free with your cuffing and kicking." Stepping over Will, the captain started up the ladder. "Stay alongside with the boat," he told the seamen. "If I can find none to claim the lad, ye'll row him ashore."

Will started to yell, "Mr. Carver!" but thought better of it. Instead, he hastily thrust the bundle of books into his sea bag, tied the birdcage to it and hung the lot over his shoulder. He was up the ladder like a squirrel before the sailors could stop him.

A moment later, he tumbled on deck. He almost tripped Captain Jones, who gave a startled roar and

at once leaned over the rail to tongue-lash the seamen for letting him get away from them.

Will grabbed his sea bag, prepared to run, when two strange boys suddenly blocked his way. One was eight or nine and the other a couple of years younger.

"You don't belong here!" declared the older brother.

"There's no room for you," said the younger one. "The ship's full."

"Get out of my way!" Will cried in panic, making a rush at them.

Instantly, the brothers leaped upon him. Boys, sea bag, and birdcage came down with a terrific thud.

Just then two paws, big as a bear's, picked up the brothers by their jerkins and stood them on their feet. And Will found himself staring up at the angry face of Captain Jones.

"A fine thing!" growled Jones. "You're no sooner aboard than you get into a fight. Boys fighting. Girls crying. Children everywhere. I'm not a skipper, I'm a blasted nursemaid!"

"Will! Will, what's the trouble?" they heard. And Mr. Carver came striding up.

"Oh, Mr. Carver!" Will cried. "I've had a terrible time getting aboard. I was almost left behind."

"I know, I know," Mr. Carver interrupted him, soothingly. "Thank you, Captain, for bringing him."

The skipper muttered ungraciously, "Hope he's no

troublemaker like the Billington boys. I don't need another one, with them two."

He turned to Mr. Carver and asked gruffly, "Well, seeing ye found your apprentice, sir, are ye all aboard?"

"Yes, I believe I can account for all the Pilgrims," Mr. Carver replied. "Let's see," he began, thinking aloud. "Counting those from the *Speedwell,* who had come from Leyden, Holland, and the ones who remained on the *Mayflower* . . . that makes forty-one. Yes, forty-one Pilgrims. You must have the count of the Strangers, Captain Jones."

At that, the captain burst out laughing. "So that's what ye Pilgrims call the others – Strangers!" he exclaimed. "Why, sir, they're all Englishmen, same as ye. Loyal subjects of King James of England."

"We call them Strangers, Captain, only because they are not of our religious faith," Mr. Carver explained.

"Well," said Jones, "Saints ye may call yourselves. And Strangers, ye may call the others. But, as for me, I call the lot of ye, passengers. And, counting this boy, there's one hundred and two of ye. And forty-one of the number are children or maids and lads about the age of this young sprout, Will. Did you know that, Mr. Carver? A blooming nursery! And hear this, sir, keep them out of the way of my crew or I'll . . ."

The captain's threat was cut short by Elizabeth Tilley and a crowd of children, charging towards them down the deck.

"Zij is Will! It is Will!" Elizabeth was crying. She tried to speak English always as her father and mother wanted her to. But, whenever she was excited, her speech became a curious mixture of English and the Dutch they learned in Holland.

Over the excited exclamations they heard Captain Jones thunder, "All hands! Weigh anchor!"

Will wedged himself in among the passengers, who were waving good-bye to the people of Plymouth. Tears came into his eyes as the sails were spread, all shining and white, and the *Mayflower* began to move slowly out of the harbor.

"Mit de hulp van een Providence," said Elizabeth softly, her own heart too full to remember her English.

"Yes, with the help of Providence," Will repeated in a whisper, "this time I will really get to see America."

SEASICK

"WILL, I think I've got my sea legs," Giles Hopkins remarked one day when the *Mayflower* was some eight hundred miles out on the ocean. "The smell doesn't bother me at all any more."

Will sniffed the strong odor of the chicken coop and the pen for pigs and goats, which they were cleaning. He did not feel queasy.

"Hooray!" he shouted. "I feel fine! The smell doesn't bother me, either."

Will and Giles Hopkins, the teen-age son of one of the families of Strangers, had struck up a friendship. When the Pilgrim leaders assigned work, it had fallen to Will and Giles to look after the livestock. They had even taken turns cleaning the pens and being seasick.

Today, they felt so good, they climbed up to the crow's-nest at the top of the mainmast. They clung to the ropes as the mast swung them back and forth. It was like riding a great pendulum. The sailor on lookout up there let them look through his brass spyglass.

"And beyond the horizon, somewhere over in that direction," the sailor told them, pointing to the west, "lies Virginia in America." After a while, Will and Giles climbed down.

Presently, John Billington, the younger brother,

came up on deck. He had been sick for the past week. He could not eat for vomiting. This morning he crawled as far as the main hatch and sat down to watch Will and Giles.

"Good morning, John. Glad you're feeling better," Will greeted him cheerily.

"Bah!" said John. He got up and tottered off in the direction of the forecastle. The ship's crew lived there.

The next thing Will and Giles knew, John came flying out shrieking, "Don't! Don't! Don't!"

Hard on his heels, flourishing a belaying pin, was the rough sailor. The boys called him The Meanun.

Will dashed forward, grasped John's arm and swung the boy behind him. "Don't you dare touch him!" he warned The Meanun.

"Then let him stay aft where he belongs," the sailor declared in an ugly tone. "Next time he comes a-prying about the crew's quarters, he'll get a clout alongside the head. And that goes for the rest of ye!"

Then they noticed John. He was turning green. They hustled him to the rail. Will held John's head, while John fed the fishes.

"Disgustin' people, these Pilgrims," muttered The Meanun as he left. "They and their younguns pukin' all over the ship. I'll see half of them buried before this voyage is over. I'll live to enjoy the goods they leave behind."

Burial at Sea: The mean sailor who cursed the Pilgrims became ill and quickly died. The Pilgrims took part in the solemn funeral service. His body, sewn in canvas, goes into the icy sea.

"You'll live to be hanged," Will shouted after him angrily, "if you keep on bullying people."

"I only sat down in there with The Meanun," explained John as soon as he felt better, "because I was afraid I was going to be sick again. You see, I thought it all out. None of the sailors got sick. So the forecastle must be the place where you can't get seasick."

"Who told you there was such a place?" Will asked.

"I did," said Francis Billington, suddenly appearing. He gave his brother a look of disgust. "John shouldn't be a big ninny and believe a silly thing."

Francis had a stick gun on his shoulder. Now he quickly aimed it at them and roared out, "Bang! You're all dead!"

"You quit that!" his brother cried. "I don't like being shot at."

"Give me that gun," Will commanded, making a grab to take the stick gun away.

"You'll have to catch me!" Francis declared. He ran fast as a deer down the deck.

He ran headlong into Captain Myles Standish, the Pilgrims' military commander. Captain Standish was just coming on deck. It was time to drill the Pilgrims in the use of their muskets.

Francis had almost upset him, and the Captain's

quick temper flared. "Get up there on the poop deck," he barked at Francis. "You, too, up there!" he told Will and Giles, pointing at the high deck at the stern of the ship. "I don't want any of you boys down here during drill, understand?"

CAPTAIN SHRIMP

THE voice of Captain Myles Standish rang out over the deck. "HA-LT! FRONT FACE!"

The Pilgrim men faced the little, red-haired, fighting cock of a soldier.

"Now, we are going to load and fire our muskets as fast as possible," Standish explained. "Now, get everything ready," he continued as though he were teaching a class of children. "Have your powder handy, gentlemen – shot, ramrod – everything."

The Pilgrims fingered their guns gingerly. Many

fumbled getting their shot bags open. Others struggled with their powder horns. Standish watched them, biting his lips with impatience.

Up on the poop deck the boys leaned on the rail and observed all that went on below.

"Take charge of the boys and see they behave themselves," Captain Standish told Will and Giles earlier. "When you boys get to racketing about up

there with your stick guns, it disturbs the men drilling."

So far, Will and Giles had succeeded in keeping the boys quiet. The smaller boys wriggled and kept asking, "When are we going to fire our muskets? Why can't we play we're fighting Indians, like we did the other day?"

And Giles said, "Captain's orders. We must keep still and watch today." And the boys obeyed.

Now from the deck below, the boys heard Captain Standish give the command:

"LOAD!"

They saw the men begin to ram powder and shot into their muskets.

In a few moments, a cry like a wail rose from Standish. "No, no, gentlemen! Faster! You must work faster. Suppose Indians are attacking. Before you get your guns loaded, they'll lift your scalps."

"But, sir, we Pilgrims know little or nothing of firearms," one of the men said plaintively. "You must be patient with us."

"Patient! I have been patient. I am patient," snapped the short-tempered commander. "You must work faster!"

The boys became bored and restless watching the men. Even Will and Giles felt they were taking a very long time. They were unbelievably clumsy, too.

The cook in his galley.

Captain Standish's already red face grew redder and redder. No wonder the boys called him "Captain Shrimp." He certainly looked like a boiled shrimp, with his fiery hair, red face, and being small to boot.

"Mr. Carver!" cried Standish. "You are spilling powder on the deck. Put it in the gun, sir!"

He waited a moment, then bellowed, "Ready! FIRE!"

There was a smattering of cracks and pops. Then one musket went off with a terrific roar.

As though set off by the musket fire, the boys yelled at the top of their voices, "BANG! BANG! BANG, BANG, BANG!"

Then Francis Billington shouted, "Capture 'em!" And he and a group of shrieking boys lunged at Giles Hopkins and threw him down.

At once the air was filled with screaming, yelling, shouting. All the morning's bottled-up energy exploded.

"Shooting sun" with cross-staff to fix ship's position.

A group of boys went tearing down the steps to the big deck. They yelped happily, "We're Indians! We're going to scalp everybody! We're wild Indians."

Will tore after them to try to stop them. As they all neared the waist of the ship, Captain Standish stepped out, waving them down. Grabbing Will by the front of his jerkin, he whirled him about.

"What's the meaning of this racket?" Standish

demanded. "I thought I told you and Giles . . ."

"I know, sir," Will said. "I know we were in charge. But they sort of got out of control, sir, all of a sudden."

Mr. Carver and some of the men joined the group.

"I can't put Will and Giles in charge of the others again," Standish said. "They'll have to learn first how to keep the younger boys in hand."

"You boys had all better go below and stay there for the rest of the day," said Mr. Carver. "We'll have no more make-believe fighting between white men and Indians. We are going to America to make our homes, not make war on the natives."

MAN OVERBOARD

IN the darkness of the 'tween deck, Will sat with a group of men and boys listening with frightened ears to the gale howling outside. And they ate their cold supper of boiled salt beef and hard dry biscuit.

Will could scarcely remember his last hot meal. The storm had started when they were about halfway across the ocean. Since then, they had lived in the dark belly of the pitching ship.

Will smelled the stench of unwashed bodies, rotting food, and the *Mayflower's* former cargoes of fish, turpentine and tar. It was overpowering.

"I can't breathe in here," John Howland, Mr. Carver's secretary, said suddenly.

One lurch, more violent than the other, suddenly threw Will to the floor. His head throbbed from a bang against a stanchion. Icy water dripped down on him. He was paralyzed with fear.

Will heard a sharp gasp of pain near him. And John Howland said loudly, "We must have a light to see to lash things down. It's dangerous to have them crashing about. I've already hurt my leg."

Will found a dry candle in his sea bag. Howland struck a spark and lighted the candle.

"We'd best get some lanterns," one of the men said.

Will strained at ropes to secure the vinegar kegs. Beside him he could hear Howland's labored breathing.

"You had better rest," Will told him.

"I'll be all right," Howland answered. "I can't catch my breath. I must get some air." In another moment, he staggered off.

Frightened, Will went after him. He lost Howland

for a time in the shadows. Then Will saw him climbing the ladder. Howland pushed the hatch open. Water cascaded down as he stepped to the deck.

"Mr. Howland! Mr. Howland! Come back!" Will shouted. The man must have taken leave of his senses to go out on the open deck in the storm.

Will scurried up the ladder. Just as he raised his head above the opening, a great wave swept past. To his horror, he heard Howland cry, "Help! Help! Somebody help me!"

"Man overboard!" Will screamed. "Mr. Howland's washed overboard!"

Sailors came running. They brought ropes and tied them about their waists.

"Howland! Howland!" a sailor called out. "Listen. Listen, I thought I heard something."

"The water's icy. No one can stay alive in it," another said.

Then Captain Jones roared, "Quiet! Listen everybody. Men," he called to his crew, "swing your lanterns over the side. Search the water."

For a moment there was nothing to be heard but the storm's roar. Then Will caught a thin, wild cry.

"I heard him! I heard Howland!" Will screamed. "He's down this way!"

Two sailors swung their lanterns in wide arcs.

"There he is!" one of them cried. "He's hanging on to one of the halyards."

"Bear a hand, men!" Captain Jones bellowed.

Hands grasped the halyard. Men hauled it in.

"Use your boathook," Jones commanded a sailor.

Will watched them catch Howland's jerkin with the hook and pull him out, gasping and shivering.

"Thank God," said Carver. "Thank God, he's saved!"

DANGER!

THE storm went on day after day. And the wind blew without rest, day and night. The ship, bare of sails, wallowed helplessly.

Cold, wet, hungry, the Pilgrims listened in terror as the waves dashed against the ship as if to tear it apart. With the roaring and hissing of a cataract, water cascaded over the deck.

One night, when the storm was at its worst, they heard a tremendous cracking of wood overhead.

"What's that terrible noise?" several cried.

"The beam! The beam!" someone answered.

Will leaped from his bunk and hurried with the others to the middle of the ship. A lantern cast light overhead. They looked up. The main crossbeam of the ship had a great crack in it. It sagged dangerously.

They heard voices shouting from somewhere above them. In a moment, they saw Captain Jones come down the ladder with the carpenter and several seamen.

"Stand aside," Jones ordered the Pilgrims. "Let the carpenter have a look."

They waited fearfully while the carpenter examined the beam by the light of a lantern. They saw him shake his head. "That beam is badly cracked."

"If it breaks," declared one of the seamen, "we'll all drown. The sea will crush the ship like an eggshell."

The Pilgrims listened in dread as quick mutterings broke out among the crew. – "can't be repaired," – "best put back to England," – "we'll all be drowned."

"Avast!" Jones cried. "What say ye, carpenter? Can ye repair it or not?"

"Braced with a great, stout post, the beam would hold," replied the man.

"But ye know we've no way to lift the beam," Jones told him angrily.

"She's strong and firm under water, sir," the carpenter reminded the skipper."

"Ay, she's that," said Jones. "But she's not safe with

a cracked main beam. It's got to be lifted up."

Lifted? But with what? Into Will's mind flashed the memory of the great iron thing he had seen deep in the hold. The Pilgrims had brought it from Holland. It was put under heavy loads to lift them up.

What was Mr. Fletcher saying? "Great iron jackscrew."

That was it. The jackscrew!

"I know where it's stowed, sir!" Will burst out.

Will led the sailors down into the gloomy cavern of the hold. There, in the deepest part of the ship, among the cannon, anvils, and grindstones, Will found the great jackscrew.

Staggering under the weight of the jackscrew, two sailors brought it up. They set it under the beam. The sailors started to turn up the jack. It pressed against the wood. There was a creaking sound, but the beam did not move. Will caught his breath. Was the jack strong enough to lift the oak beam?

The sailors turned the screw again. Will saw it slowly rise, screeching at every turn. Little by little it pushed the great beam back into place. The jack held the beam there firmly.

A great sigh escaped the watchers.

"There's no longer danger," said Captain Jones.

LAND HO!

THE weather did not get any worse, but it did not get much better. Seams in the upper deck had opened. At times the water rose ankle deep in the 'tween deck.

When that happened Mr. Carver called out, "Buckets!" The boys brought buckets from everywhere. They bailed along with the men, passing the buckets from hand to hand to the two boys stationed at the open porthole. It was back-breaking work.

Suddenly the weather cleared, followed by the warmth of late October.

"My father thinks Captain Jones is taking us far out of our way," Giles said to Will. "We've been sailing almost two months. My father says we should be in Virginia by now."

"But we've had storms. We were blown off our course," Will reminded them.

There was a derisive snort from the sailor next to them. "Storms or no storms, we should be ashore by now," he declared. "If," he paused to emphasize his next words, "we had headed in the right direction.

But it don't look to me like we're heading for Virginia."

"I suppose you've been there before, sir," Will said, bristling.

"No. But I've been matey with them what has," replied the sailor.

Will refused to believe him. But the ship lumbered on and on. And it grew cold.

Was this the warm Virginia climate Mr. Carver was always talking about?

Then at dawn on November 10, he was wakened by a cry which rang through the ship. "LAND HO!"

There was a great rush of feet across the deck. He could hear people hurrying from their cabins and from all parts of the ship. He reached the deck just in time to join Giles and the other boys scrambling up into the rigging. The Pilgrims lined the rail.

As the morning fog lifted they saw, not far away, high red cliffs. Land!

The lookout in the top cried suddenly, "Breakers ahead!"

And he heard Captain Jones shout orders.

"Hard a starboard the helm!" he roared.

The helmsman pulled the tiller.

"What's the matter? What has happened?" the Pilgrims cried.

"The ship was headed for the breakers," Captain Jones answered. "She'd have killed herself on the shoals."

Breathlessly, Will watched the ship turn away from the rough water. The bow of the *Mayflower* swung around. The ship headed back up the coast. She rounded the curve of a cape into a fine harbor.

The land was bleak. The winter wind was icy cold. Was this land Virginia?

"Let go the anchor!" commanded Jones.

With a great rattle of chains, the anchor plunged to the bottom. The *Mayflower* came to rest.

Mr. Carver, Mr. Brewster and Mr. Bradford joined

At Provincetown they all signed the Mayflower Compact

Mr. Hopkins and Captain Jones. They talked earnestly together. Then Will saw the captain put his speaking trumpet to his lips.

"Hear this, all you passengers," he called out. "This land is not the place we sailed for. It is not Virginia. Blown out of our course, we have landed far to the north. We are in New England, as John Smith, the great explorer, named it on his map. We don't rightly know who, if anyone, lays claim to this land."

"Hooray! Hooray!" shouted Mr. Billington. Several other men cheered loudly.

"It's every man for himself," cried Mr. Billington. "No country has a hold on us now."

"He's right!"

"We're free to do as we please!"

"We'll do away with governors! And all the old laws!"

The rest were silent, stunned by the threatening tones of Billington and his companions. Then Mr. Bradford spoke up.

"What you men suggest is anarchy. We must have some form of government or we are all lost."

There was a burst of protest.

"Silence!" shouted Mr. Bradford. "We must not snarl at one another like a pack of dogs. Let all the men gather in the big cabin and agree upon how we shall govern ourselves."

The group of rebellious men greeted his words with growling and black looks.

"Come along, all of you," urged Mr. Bradford. "You must all have a part in making a compact."

He entered the big cabin, followed by a large group of the men.

The others are not going, Will thought.

Then, slowly and grudgingly, one by one, the rebels filed into the cabin.

The Mayflower Compact

In the name of God, amen. We, whose names are underwritten, the loyal subjects of our dread Sovereign Lord King James, by the grace of God, of Great Britain, France, and Ireland, King, defender of the faith, &c. Having undertaken for the glory of God, and advancement of the Christian faith, and the honour of our King and country, a voyage to plant the first colony in the northern parts of Virginia; do by these presents, solemnly and mutually in the presence of God and one another, covenant and combine ourselves together into a civil body politick, for our better ordering and preservation, and furtherance of the ends aforesaid; and by virtue hereof do enact, constitute, and frame, such just and equal laws, ordinances, acts, constitutions, and offices, from time to time, as shall be thought most meet and convenient for the general good of the colony; unto which we promise all due submission and obedience.

ADVENTURE ON THE CAPE

NEXT morning Will was straightening up his bunk, when he heard, "Will! Will, bundle yourself in warm clothes. A party is going ashore. Governor Carver wants you to go with them."

Will looked at John Howland, muffled to the ears.

"Governor Carver wants me? *Governor,* did you say?" Will asked, surprised.

"That's right. *Governor* Carver," replied Howland heartily. "We men signed a compact. As loyal subjects of King James of England, we agreed to set up a government with just and equal laws for all. Even the rebels – Mr. Billington and the rest – all signed! Mr. Carver was made governor of the new colony." Howland started off. "Now, hurry."

Going ashore! Will snatched up his leather jerkin. He started down the passageway only to find it blocked by people, spilling out of the White's cabin. To Will's annoyance, everybody insisted, "Will, you must see the new baby."

Nothing would do but he had to peer at the little thing in its cradle while Resolved, its brother, held up a lantern.

"Our first baby born in America," Mrs. White said proudly. "We named the little traveler Peregrine."

Will murmured that it was a fine looking baby and got away as quickly as he could.

On deck, all was a bustle of people working. The carpenter worked on repair of the shallop. Then the struggling crew hoisted the Pilgrims' boat through the main hatchway and into the water.

In another part of the ship, seamen strained at ropes to lower the longboat. Nearby, Captain Standish, Mr. Carver, and fifteen or so others, armed with muskets, busily tied powder horns and bags of shot to their belts.

Women darted about with bags of food, scarves and mitts for the men and children going ashore. The longboat settled with a splash in the water. And Captain Standish called out, "All those in the shore party, get into the boat."

They pulled away. Soon they brought up on Cape

A baby is born and named Peregrine White

Cod beach, less than a mile from the ship. Will, Giles and the other children leaped out. Oh, to be on land again! They raced up and down, shouted, rolled, tussling in the sand.

"You've played enough," Governor Carver told them presently. "While we explore the place, you boys gather firewood. The sailors will dig a fresh-water well in the sand. When you have a supply of wood and water, return with it to the ship."

Cries of disappointment burst from the boys. "Please, let us go with you, sir," Will begged.

Carver shook his head. And the exploring party set off along the shore with Captain Standish marching ahead. The sailors disappeared among the sand dunes to dig for water. The boys were left alone.

For the first time, they had a good look around. Cape Cod was terribly still after the creaking, groaning ship. And big! The sandy beach stretched as far as the eye could reach. Back of it for miles dark pines and wind-crippled oaks rose above thick underbrush. It struck them, of a sudden, that they were going to live in this vast, lonely wilderness. They began to remember tales they had been told of strange beasts in the American forests. And red Indians!

And they almost jumped out of their skins as a rabbit leaped from a nearby thicket and vanished among the dunes. They laughed weakly. They had fully expected it to be a bear. On legs wobbly from months on heaving decks, the boys set about picking up driftwood and lugging it to the longboat.

Will wandered farther and farther away in his search for wood. Then, led on by finding crab and

lobster shells, he began to look for other shellfish. Among the rocks, he discovered mussels. He sampled several, finding they tasted delicious. But after he had eaten them, he had a pain in his stomach, so he ate no more.

Just then a queer sort of waterbird, flying low over a marsh, attracted his attention. He pushed through the underbrush to watch it.

Before he knew it, he was in a small valley between high sand dunes. He saw little mounds of sand. Curious to know what was in them, he began digging. He dug for a time without discovering anything. Then

his fingers touched something solid. Soon he uncovered a basket filled with red, yellow, and blue ears of Indian corn.

What a story he would have to tell the others!

Thrusting as many ears as he could manage in the front of his jerkin, he stood up. Then he sank down again quickly, behind the heap of sand. Several Indians, bright feathers bobbing on their heads, were moving at a jog trot through scrub pine woods.

They had a dog with them and it suddenly darted away in chase of some small animal. Then Will saw a squirrel come bounding toward him across the meadow, with the dog after it. He crouched stone-still.

One of the Indians, seeing the dog about to lose the squirrel, raised his bow and sent an arrow whizzing through the air. It felled the squirrel.

With a bound, the dog leaped upon the kill. He started to pick it up, paused, lifted his head and began to sniff the air suspiciously. He had caught a strange scent. The wind was in the right direction for him to be able to follow it straight to Will.

The landing party finds corn buried by Indians. This corn later saved Pilgrim lives.

With his heart thumping like a drum, Will backed away as fast and silently as he could manage. While the dog was busy smelling at the mound of sand, Will turned and ran. He ran faster than he had ever run before. He did not care where he went, so long as it was away from the Indians. Tales of scalpings flashing through his mind, and added speed to tired feet and legs.

After a while, the thunder of waves brought him up short. He had come out to the water's edge. On he went, running and walking, running and walking. Finally, he stumbled, fell, and was unable to get up again. Past caring any longer, he crawled behind a sand dune and lay there.

JOURNEY'S END

THE next thing he knew, it was almost dark. And men were shouting. Then he saw Captain Standish and Mr. Carver.

He heard the captain say, "It's a good thing we returned by way of the beach. The lad would have frozen to death before morning. I'll signal the longboat to come fetch us."

There was the sound of the captain's musket shot.

In a little while, Will felt himself lifted into Mr. Carver's arms and being carried to the boat.

After that it was mixed and vague. He knew only that he lay sick with fever for a long time while Mrs. Carver nursed him.

As though in a dream, he heard news of the exploring parties. Of their bringing back a load of Indian corn in the shallop. Of their meeting with different Indians.

He caught snatches of conversation about the sea monsters, called whales, that were spouting and playing near the ship.

There was a day when bedding and clothes were piled in heaps, and iron pots and tubs clanged and clattered as the women prepared to hold a great washday on the beach.

Days later, Will realized they were sailing to some other place, for he was aware again of the rolling, pitching movement of the ship.

One morning, he opened his eyes to find his head quite clear. He lay, listening for the sounds of people stirring about. But the ship was strangely empty and silent. It seemed almost deserted.

Alarmed, he swung his legs to the floor. After a number of trials, he found he could stand, then move about on his trembling legs. He walked a bit and strength gradually returned to them. Wrapped in a shawl, he tottered into the passage. On his way outside, he met no one. At first, he thought there was

no one on deck, either.

Then up in the bow he saw four of the Pilgrim men on watch. And at the far end of the ship, he had a glimpse of sailors, fishing over the stern.

He noticed a moment later a lone figure, swathed in a blanket, leaning upon the rail. It was Giles! With closed eyes and uplifted face, Giles was praying.

A terrible fear took hold of Will. What had happened to all the others? Were the few on the ship all that was left of the Pilgrim company?

He was on the point of crying out, when he chanced to look toward shore. There a solemn sight met his eyes. The Pilgrims were all on the beach! They were praying. Why were they praying?

Will went over and stood beside Giles.

"Dear Lord, we thank Thee from our hearts for Thy goodness in bringing us safe to this fair place," Giles was whispering. "We thank Thee for guiding us to new Plymouth, in America, with its great abundance of good things for our new colony. We thank Thee for this place in this new land where we can dwell in peace and make our homes . . ."

Gazing out upon the long beach, the rich land and the dark woods of pine and birch, Will felt peace come into his heart. "Here we shall make our homes" he murmured. "And follow in the ways of the Lord all the days of our lives. Amen."

Will Latham survived the first dreadful winter. Six years later the town meeting voted him one-eighth share in the "great White-back Cow's" calf. In 1643 he joined a colonist group to settle the Bahama Islands. Will and the entire colony died of starvation.